APT
GL

The Bunny family came home to find
a bundle outside their door.

They peeked. They gasped. It was a baby wolf!
"He's adorable!" said Mama. "He's ours!" said Papa.

WOLFIE

THE BUNNY

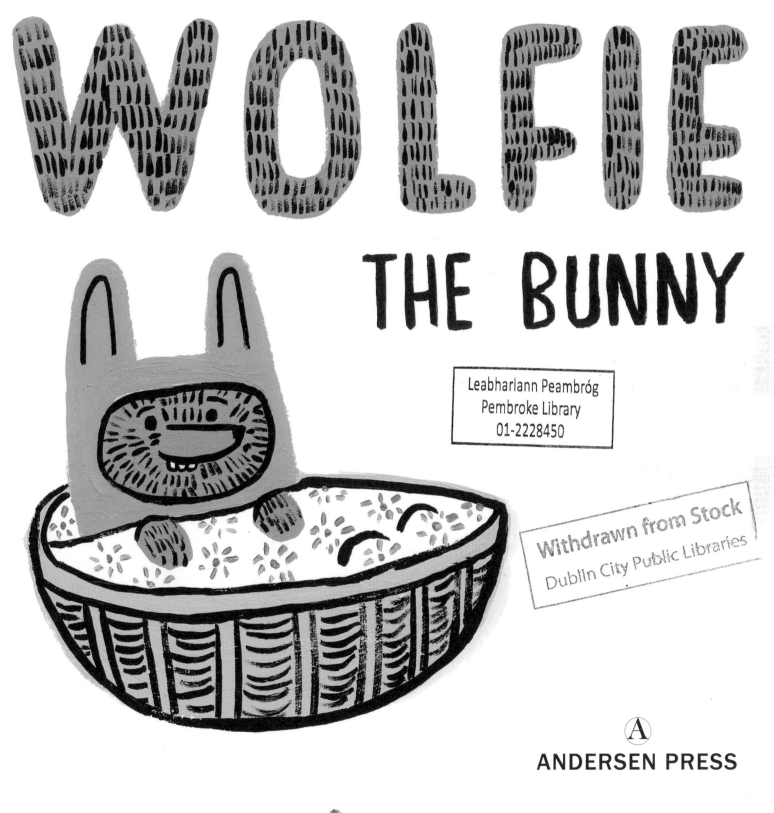

Ⓐ
ANDERSEN PRESS

Written by **Ame Dyckman** Illustrated by **Zachariah OHora**

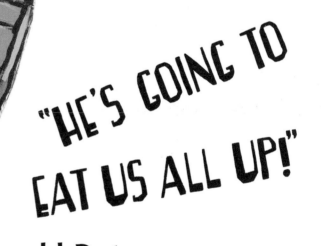

"HE'S GOING TO EAT US ALL UP!"

said Dot.

But Mama and Papa were too smitten to listen.

Wolfie slept through the night.

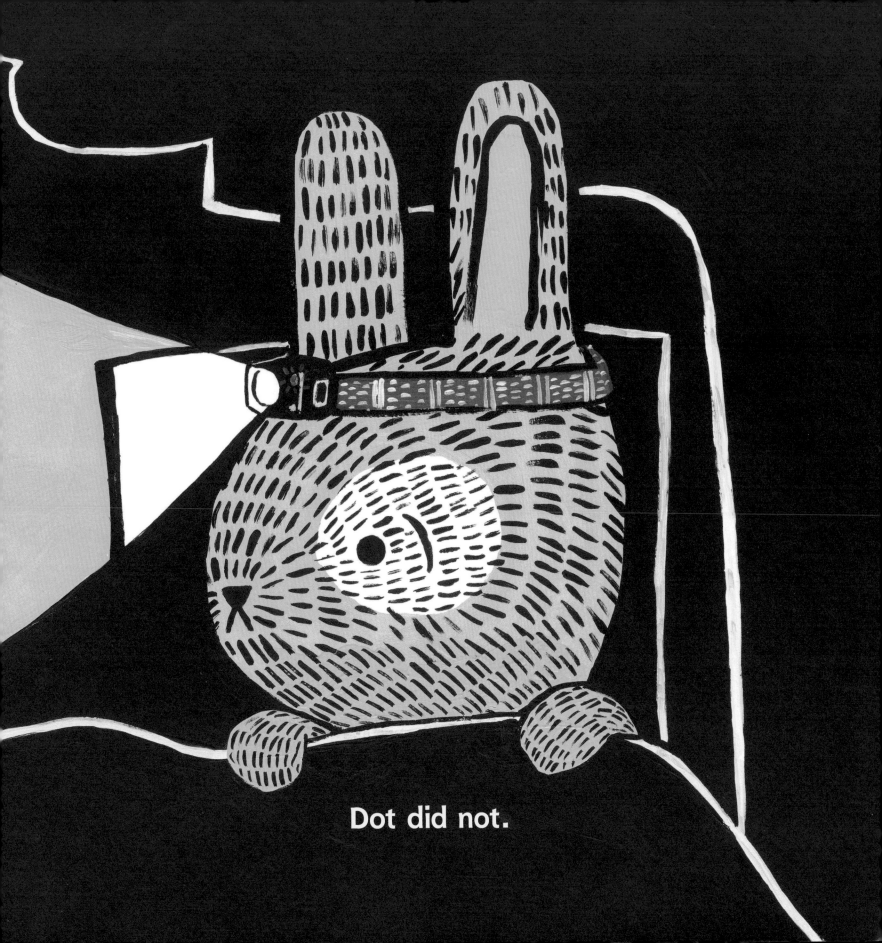

Dot did not.

Mama served carrots for breakfast.
"He likes them!" said Mama.

"He's a good eater!" said Papa.

"Speaking of eating," said Dot,

"HE'S GOING TO EAT US ALL UP!"

But Mama and Papa were too busy
taking pictures to listen.

Dot's friends came by to see the baby.

"He's sleeping," whispered Mama.
"He's a good sleeper," whispered Papa.

"HE'S GOING TO EAT US ALL UP!"

they screamed.

"Yep," said Dot.
"Let's play at your house."

For the first time, Wolfie cried.

But Dot was too far away to hear him.

When Dot returned,
Wolfie was waiting.

Everywhere Dot went,
Wolfie went, too.

"He's dribbling on me!"
said Dot.

"He's a good dribbler!"
said Papa.

The days passed, and Wolfie grew.
So did his appetite.

When Mama opened the cupboard, she got a surprise.
"The carrots!" said Mama. "They're gone!"
"Oh no!" said Papa.

"HE ATE THEM ALL UP!"

said Dot.

Dot fetched the carrot bag.
But she did not get far.

Wolfie and Dot went to the Carrot Patch.

Dot was picking one last carrot when Wolfie's mouth opened wide.

"I *knew* it!" cried Dot.

"On guard!"

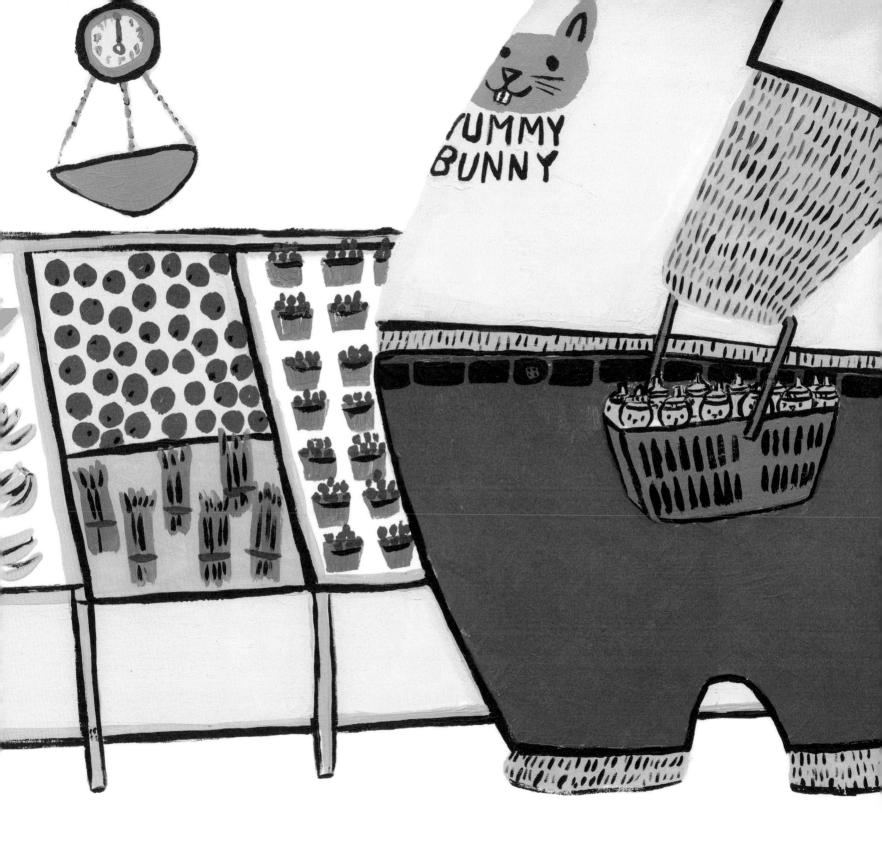

But Wolfie wasn't looking at Dot.

"DINNER!"

roared the bear.

It was Dot's chance to run away.

Instead, she ran forward.

"Let him go!" Dot demanded.

"Or... I'LL EAT YOU ALL UP!"

The bear blinked. "You're a bunny," he said.

"I'M A HUNGRY BUNNY," said Dot.

"But I'm bigger than you,"
said the bear.

"I'LL START ON YOUR TOES,"
said Dot.

Dot relaxed as the bear ran away.
"We're safe!" she said.

Then Wolfie pounced.

"Come on, little brother.
Let's go home and eat."

For Kaia, my Wolf Baby.
– A.D.

For the Kitten, the O Bear,
the Twookie,
and also for Marlow's
mum and dad – L.D.D.
– Z.O.

First published in Great Britain in 2016 by Andersen Press Ltd.,
20 Vauxhall Bridge Road, London SW1V 2SA.
Originally published by Little, Brown and Company, Hachette Book Group,
1290 Avenue of the Americas, New York, NY 10104, USA
Copyright © Little, Brown and Company
Text copyright © 2015 by Ame Dyckman
Illustrations copyright © 2015 by Zachariah OHora
The rights of Ame Dyckman and Zachariah OHora to be identified as
the author and illustrator of this work have been asserted by them
in accordance with the Copyrights, Designs and Patents Act, 1988.
All rights reserved.
Printed and bound in China.

5 7 9 10 8 6 4

British Library Cataloguing in Information Data available.

ISBN 978 1 78344 387 1